The Snowflake

We have only this moment, sparkling
like a star in our hand – and
melting like a snowflake...
– Sir Francis Bacon

For my dad, who inspired
this story – the real Pappie

The
Snowflake

Benji Davies

HarperCollins *Children's Books*

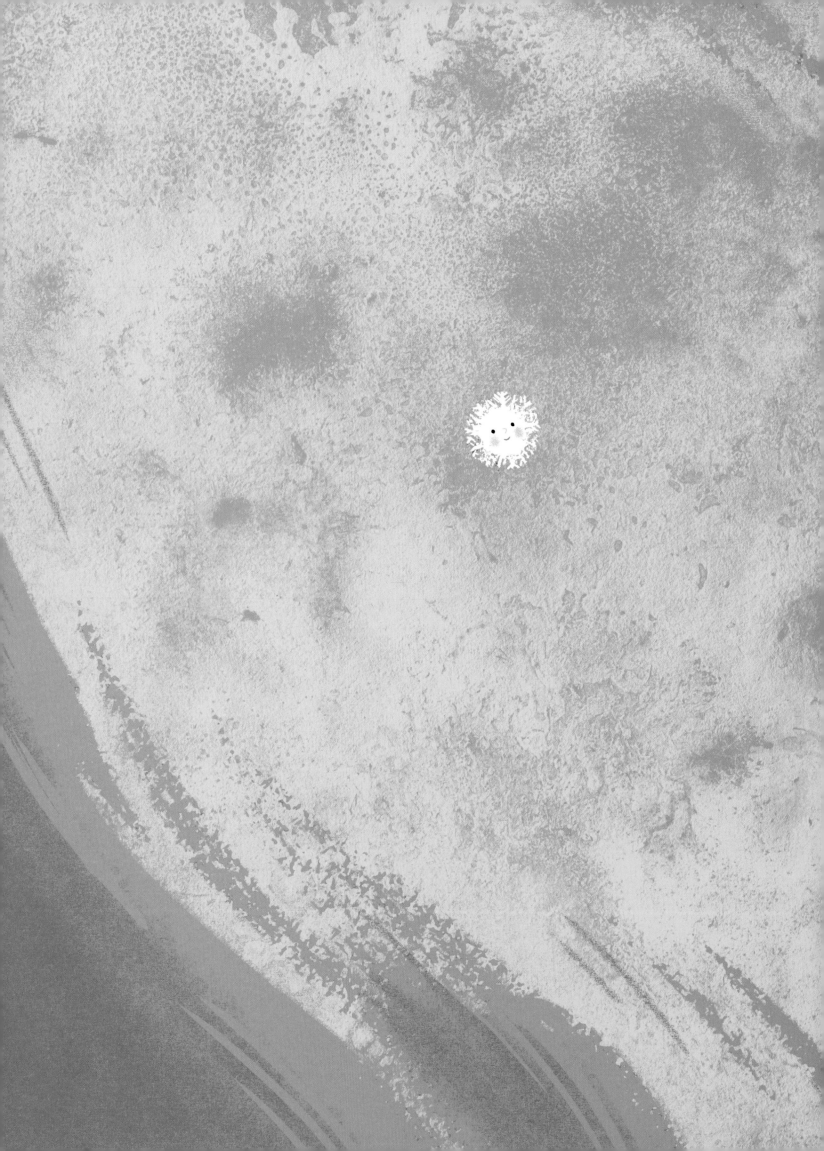

High in the sky, one winter's night,
a snowflake was made.

She wheeled and skipped and twirled
between the clouds.

"Wheeeeeeee!" she squealed.

Only soon she began to fall.

"But I don't want to fall!" said the snowflake.

"You're supposed to fall," said a cloud.
"That's what snowflakes do."

"But I don't want to!" pleaded the snowflake.
"Help me, Cloud. Stop me from falling!"

"You'll find your way…" replied the cloud. "Good luck!"

The snowflake wasn't at all sure.
She twisted this way and that way…
that way and this way.

Tumbling as she fell, the snowflake grew dizzy.

Far away in a town nestled between the hills,
a little girl called Noelle and her grandpa, Pappie,
were walking home.

Noelle's breath puffed into the cold, crisp air.

I wonder if it will snow tonight, she thought.

The snowflake fell over tree-dotted hillsides.
She drifted over valleys and streams.
She hoped she would soon stop falling...

...when she came upon a place that looked promising.

But every time she thought she was about to land...

the wind whisked the snowflake onwards.

There was nothing she could do.

She passed many windows that glowed through the evening light.

In one window sat a tree strung with lights,
and on top a bright star shimmered.

For a moment, the snowflake forgot
all about falling.

Oh, to be the star on
that glistening little tree!
she thought.

Noelle saw that window too. The tree was decorated
in every colour, and on top its star shone brightly.

Noelle wished she had a tree like that.
"Maybe next year," Pappie said.

They passed many more windows with trees in them,
each one different, each one beautiful.

Then, not far from home, Noelle found a branch beside the path.

"My own little tree!"
she said.

High above, the air grew colder, the sky grew darker, the wind
blew harder... and the snowflake rushed along with it.

She wondered if she would ever find a place to land.

Then through the wind she heard laughter…

There were more like her, more snowflakes!
They danced and swirled in the night air together.

They were joined by even more snowflakes that
rushed along, in and out and around one another.

They were never next to each other for very long
and each snowflake was different.

But, one way or another, they were all falling
and this made the snowflake feel much better.

When Noelle arrived home,
she set to work.

Her mummy took down some old
boxes and paper and, together with
Pappie, Noelle decorated the tree.

They used all the different
colours just like the tree
in the window.

They made some paper
snowflakes too.

Noelle put the tree outside where she could see it.

She hoped that its little branches might soon
be covered with *real snow*.

But as Noelle went up to bed she felt that there was
something else missing from her tree.

Something important.
Only she wasn't quite sure what it was.

High above the house, the sky was swirling…
drifting…
circling…
falling…

"Nearly there!"
whispered the cloud.

When Noelle woke the next morning,
the world felt different.

Everything was brighter,
quieter, softer.

Then as she climbed out of bed
she remembered...

"My little tree!" she said.

And Noelle gasped!

For every rooftop, every hillside and every tree had grown white.

One special snowflake had
settled on the very top of Noelle's little tree.

"I did it!" said the snowflake. "I found a way to stop falling!"

And she felt very proud.

Noelle danced into the morning light.

The snowflake caught the sun brightly
and shone like a star.

First published in Great Britain by HarperCollins *Children's Books* in 2020
HarperCollins *Children's Books* is a division of HarperCollins*Publishers* Ltd,
HarperCollins Publishers, 1 London Bridge Street, London SE1 9GF

1 3 5 7 9 10 8 6 4 2

ISBN 978–0–00–821281–0

Benji Davies asserts the moral right to be identified as the author and illustrator of the work.

A CIP catalogue record for this title is available from the British Library.

Printed and bound in China

www.harpercollins.co.uk